Zelda and Ivy

Zelda and Ivy

LAURA McGEE KVASNOSKY

CANDLEWICK PRESS

To my sisters
Susan, Nan, and Kate,
and my brother Tim,
with love from the favorite

First paperback edition in this format 2014

The Library of Congress has cataloged the hardcover edition as follows:

Kvasnosky, Laura McGee.
Zelda and Ivy / Laura McGee Kvasnosky. — 1st ed.
p. cm.
Summary: In three brief stories, Ivy, the younger of two fox sisters, goes along with her older sister's schemes, even when they seem a bit daring.
ISBN 978-0-7636-0469-1 (hardcover)
[1. Foxes—Fiction. 2. Sisters—Fiction.] I. Title.
PZ7.K975Ze 1998
[E]—dc21   97-028179

ISBN 978-0-7636-6878-5 (reformatted paperback)

SWT 18 17 16 15 14 13
10 9 8 7 6 5 4 3 2 1

Printed in Dongguan, Guangdong, China

This book was typeset in Galliard and hand-lettered by the author-illustrator. The illustrations were done in gouache resist.

Candlewick Press
99 Dover Street
Somerville, Massachusetts 02144

visit us at www.candlewick.com

CONTENTS

Chapter One
CiRCUS aCt

"Let's play circus," said Zelda. "You can be the fabulous fox on the flying trapeze."

"Okay," said Ivy. She put on a fancy hat and sat down on the swing.

"I'm the oldest," said Zelda. "I will announce your tricks."

Zelda stepped to one side. She held out her baton.

"Behold," she said, "the fabulous Ivy on the flying trapeze."

Ivy started to swing back and forth.

She pointed her toes. She flipped her tail.

She smiled a big smile.

"And now," said Zelda, "the fabulous Ivy will stand on the flying trapeze." Ivy carefully stood up. She kept swinging back and forth.

"And now," said Zelda, "the fabulous
Ivy will stand on one paw."

Ivy stood on one paw. The swing
wobbled.

"Holding on with only one paw,"
added Zelda.

Ivy tried to hold on with only one paw.
She tried to keep smiling.

"And now," said Zelda, "the fabulous
Ivy will perform a death-defying trick:

balancing on the tip of
her tail !”

Ivy fell off the swing. She started to cry.

"Don't worry," said Zelda as she

helped her little sister dust off. "I have

trouble with that trick, too."

Chapter Two
THE LATEST STYLE

"Let's doozy up our tails like movie stars," said Zelda.

"I like my tail the way it is," said Ivy.

"It will be even more beautiful with a blue stripe," said Zelda. She reached for the paint.

"Do you really think so?" asked Ivy. She turned to see her tail in the mirror.

Zelda painted a bright blue stripe down Ivy's tail.

"The stripe brings out your natural highlights," said Zelda.

"Oh my," said Ivy. "I'm not so sure."

"Relax," said Zelda. "Stripes are cool."

"Shall I paint a stripe on your tail?" asked Ivy.

"Wait until I'm done," said Zelda. "I'm going to make your tail even better with scallops."

"Scallops?" said Ivy. "I don't know
anyone who has scallops."

Zelda cut scallops into Ivy's fluffy tail.

"Oh dear," said Ivy, trying to smooth
her tail fur.

"Don't worry," said Zelda. "Scallops are glamorous."

"Shall I scallop your tail?" asked Ivy.

"Wait until I'm done," said Zelda. "Here's the final touch." Zelda sprinkled golden glitter up and down Ivy's tail.

"Oh my," said Ivy, shaking her tail.

Zelda picked up her baton. She stepped back and pointed at Ivy.

"Voilà!" she said. "A masterpiece!"

Ivy looked down. "I kind of liked it better plain," she said.

"Plain is okay," said Zelda, "but this look is the latest style."

16

The sisters stood side by side in front of the mirror. Ivy's tail dripped paint and glitter and tufts of cut fur. Zelda's tail was fluffy and red.

Ivy picked up the scissors.

"Shall I doozy up your tail like a movie star now?" she asked.

Zelda quickly swished her tail away.

"Maybe some other time," she said. "Let's take a bubble bath."

Chapter Three
Fairy Dust

Ivy sat on the front porch and drew
stars on the screen door with her blue
crayon. Zelda marched around the yard,
twirling her baton.

"May I have a turn with your baton?"
asked Ivy.

"Not now," said Zelda. "It's still too
new for me to share."

Zelda twirled her way up the steps. She watched as Ivy colored in a very large star. Little bits of crayon piled up on the porch below the star.

"Look at this," said Zelda, picking up the crayon bits. "Magic fairy dust."

"Really?" asked Ivy.

"Oh yes," said Zelda, twitching her whiskers. "If you put this under your pillow and dream of your wish, it will come true."

Zelda marched and twirled her way back down the steps. Ivy carefully gathered the magic fairy dust.

That night Ivy put the fairy dust under her pillow.

"I wish for a baton," she said.

"It might not work the first time," said Zelda.

"A silver baton with red ribbons on the ends, just like yours," said Ivy.

"It probably lost its magic during the day," said Zelda.

"I will dream of marching and twirling just like you," said Ivy.

And she went to sleep.

But Zelda could not sleep. She looked at
her baton shining in the moonlight on the
chair. She listened to the soft snores of her
sister sleeping below her in the bunk bed.

Finally, she hopped down and quietly
put her baton next to Ivy's pillow.

In the morning when Zelda woke
up, Ivy was already marching around,
twirling the baton.

"Look, Zelda,"
she said, "my wish
came true! I have a
baton exactly like yours."

"Yes," said Zelda,
a little sadly, "exactly
like mine."

"I'm going to twirl and march all
day," said Ivy. "Get your baton and
twirl with me!"

"Oh," said Zelda. "My baton . . ."

"I'll get it for you," said Ivy. "You left it on the chair last night."

Ivy looked on the chair.

She looked under the chair.

She looked behind the chair.

Then she looked closely at the baton in her hand.

"I see," Ivy said slowly. She brushed the red ribbons against her chin.

"Zelda," she offered, "we can share my baton together."

"Thanks," said Zelda. "I am the oldest, so I will go first."